# A SOULS
# OF
# SWANS FLYING

by

Lucille and James Horner

*To Ade and Cath,*
*With warm regards and love*
*MIKE*
*25/5/2022*

# BOOK ONE

# NO SUCH LAUREATE EARTH?

## SYNOPSIS

Historical drama. This novel traces the experience of two families, one English and one South African, who are fated, despite geographical distance, to be intertwined from the beginning of the twentieth century until the present. From birth and childhood onwards, through sibling rivalry, love, ambition, loss, war, migration, endeavour, vanity, rejection, tragedy, travel, romance, civil unrest, innovation, idealism, racial issues, humour, cultural controversies, language differences, disputes over inheritance, divorce, fostering, step-families, introversion and existentialism, the characters search for ways to live, even to succeed. They must deal with the quickly changing circumstances of their time. Most significantly they must survive the indecipherable enigma that is South Africa.

Available in electronic and paper versions.

# CHAPTER TWO


# MONIKA


*by*

*James Horner*

**For**

**Elizabeth**

who would often say

"*Why* do I love you *so* much?"

## DISCLAIMER

This is a work of fiction. The story, the incidents described and the names and characters of persons in the story all originated in the writer's mind and are not based on actual people or events. Any resemblance of characters in this fiction to persons living or dead is purely coincidental. Opinions expressed by the fictitious characters are the opinions of the fictitious characters, not the opinions of the author.

ISBN: 9798408481873

# DRAMATIS PERSONAE

BELL MISS MONIKA
Wimbledon friend of Rosemary, Eric and John
Carpenter in the 1920s. Godmother to John
Carpenter.

CARPENTER MRS EILEEN, FORMERLY
GREEN, NEE MANDELSONN
Neighbour to Eric and Rosemary Carpenter. Married
Eric in later life.

CARPENTER ERIC 1879 TO 1952
Father of John Carpenter and Neil Carpenter. First
wife Rosemary. Widower. Second wife Eileen.

CARPENTER JOHN 1910 TO 2002
Father of Colin Carpenter. Colonist. Elder son of Eric
and Rosemary Carpenter. Attended Exeter College
1929 to 1932. Emigrated to South Africa 1937.

CARPENTER NEIL 1912 TO 2001
Younger son of Eric and Rosemary Carpenter.

CARPENTER MRS ROSEMARY 1880 TO 1926
Mother of John and Neil Carpenter. Wife of Eric
Carpenter.

GREEN NEILL
Son of Eileen Green.

LEECH MRS
Wimbledon friend of Monika Bell and Rosemary
Carpenter.

RICHARDS CANON
Wimbledon Anglican clergyman.

## 1927

Rosemary Carpenter's Anglican funeral in Wimbledon in the autumn of 1926 drew quite a crowd. Having been a good listener and unconsciously egalitarian, Rosemary had many friends. Her mourners came from many walks of life.

For John the day of his mother's funeral passed in a blur. He was aware of rain and tombstones and the mud of the churchyard. Being in a state of suspended animation, much of his thought was impressionistic. Some of his mother's words, however, still reverberated with clarity. "Remember this," she would say, "no matter how smart our clothes, no matter how grand our buildings, no matter how eloquent our words, we are not civilised if we do uncivilised things." Eric, John's father, stood tall at the graveside. Neil Carpenter, his brother, was present, but silent and inscrutable.

Also standing amongst those gathered at the grave, watching, was the small darkened figure of Eileen Green. She lived next door to Rosemary and Eric in an equally large house.

The soil from the newly dug grave, lying very neatly at its edge, brought eternity into focus. But eternity was, for the moment, too endless to comprehend.

"Are we really," John, in silent disbelief, asked himself, "going to leave her lying there? Just lying there? Under the rain and the sun and the wind? For ever! Under the ice in winter? In the mud? Mother? With no warmth or light? For all time? And just let the leaves fall on her?"

Much too soon they did just that. The mourners walked away. They left her.

Miss Monika Bell, Rosemary's close friend and John's godmother, put her arm around John's shoulder. Enjoining him to follow the churchyard path she coaxed him away. They walked in terrible silence amongst the low conversations of mourners. Monika was definite. She would not on this day leave John's side, not even for half a minute. Her godmothering had long since ceased, but her close friendship was engrained in the Carpenter family routine. She walked beside John the three-quarter-mile to the Carpenter home.

Over tea in Rosemary's drawing room, friends, relatives and neighbours conversed in a medley of tones. "It would," Mrs Leech, a neighbour, whispered to Monika, "require some considerable latitude with the truth to describe *her* as a mourner," Mrs Leech nudged Monika and indicated Eileen Green. Speaking quietly so as not to be overheard, she added, "I suppose she might be described as an *investor*?"

Monika, who lived at the other end of the village, agreed. "That lady knows what she wants," she said.

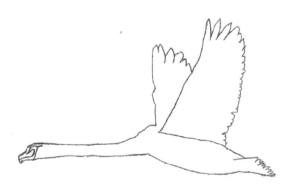

In contrast to the tranquil childhood John had known since birth, a sharp intrusion was quick to arrive. One evening in the spring of 1927, over dinner, Eric Carpenter briefly broke the sterile silence which had, in the time since Rosemary died, seeped over the joie de vivre. "In six weeks time I shall marry Eileen Green," he announced. This was all the forewarning he gave his sons of the impending union.

The boys, too unversed in the ways of the world to fully appreciate the implications of their father's statement, reacted differently.

"That's nice," Neil said blandly.

To John the announcement was a surprise as unwelcome as it is was alien. What?" he asked looking from Neil to Eric and back again.

Eric found it tedious to explain. "Eileen is going to move in with us, look after us," he said with dour impatience.

"But what about mother?" John asked.

"What about her?" Neil asked John. Neil Carpenter was a close friend of Neill Green, Eileen's son.

"Mrs Green?" John asked again.

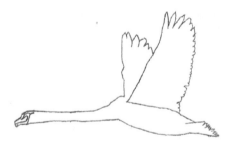

Eileen Green, assisted by her son Neill, engaged in changes that seemed natural enough to them.

"Mother, this won't do," Neill Green asserted the day after he and his mother had moved into the Carpenter house.
He stood hands on hips in the centre of the lounge, surveying everything. "This is your home now. You must make the place your own, replace all this dross with modern things, things of your own choice and liking. Everything here," he insisted, "is *so* third-estate."

"Damned nerve," John said and left the lounge.

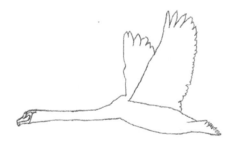

Miss Monika Bell turned up again one day. As she often did. She had tenderly promised the dying Rosemary that she would visit regularly.

Entering the garden through a spanking new gate which, in contrast to its predecessor, moved silently on new black hinges, she leaned her bicycle against the hedge as, for twenty years, she had always done. Straightening her hair and brushing off her blouse, she looked down at her all too soon-to-be middle-aged form and then up at the house. She was not altogether unhappy about the slim trim of her childlessness. But like anyone, she regretted the passage of the years.

Hoping it would be John that answered, she knocked on the door.

She was in luck. She had a keen affection for this elder son of her dead friend. "Much too keen," she sometimes admitted to herself. But with Rosemary gone she was not going to allow such thoughts to moderate her protective instinct. In the certainty that she was needed by John and that from beyond the grave Rosemary approved her actions, she kept the routine.

"Oh! Miss Bell!" John welcomed her. "I have been thinking about you and hoping you would come."

"Just stopped by to see how you are," Monika said admiring not only John as he opened the door, but also the eternal humanity he seemed to represent.

John loved Miss Bell. Already a friend while he was still in Rosemary's womb, Monika Bell had been always John's playmate and good companion. Nowadays she was also muse, sage and mentor. Miss Bell never shied away from his questions, even the awkward ones, and always gave him as much time as he needed. She had a quick understanding of needs and a discrete sense of timing. Sometimes she volunteered information and knowledge which he would later realise she must have known were relevant to his circumstances. When he reflected upon some of their conversation he felt surprise at the content. There was no-one else with whom he had ever shared thoughts about such things.

"I am very glad to see you too, my dearest," she said, kissing him on the forehead.

"You may kiss me here," she said indicating her cheek. "And now that you are seventeen, I think it time you began calling me 'Monika', don't you? Let's forget about Miss Bell."

"O.K.........Monika," John sounded her name tentatively, kissed her where indicated and processed the strangeness of acceding to the new closeness.

In the altered kitchen Monika looked about. She raised an eyebrow at the newness everywhere. But still she worked with John at making scones, as, since he was very young, she had always done. "The smell of fresh paint disturbs me," Monika said. "I don't really feel that I am working in your mother's kitchen any more. It's different. It feels a bit as if I should ask permission."

"Presumably it's still *my* kitchen, though," John answered. "So you needn't feel that way."

Over cups of tea in the lounge, Monika commented again. "New wallpaper, new carpets, new furniture, new ornaments, new paintings, new everything, and all florid," she observed.

"My mother is being swept away," John lamented. "Almost all of what we knew as her 'precious things' have gone. When Eileen and Neill moved into our house the day after the marriage, my father said they could make whatever changes they wished. And since that day change has been the only constant."

"I know dear," Monika's forehead wrinkled. "So do the village gossips."

Seeing that John was downcast, she took his hand. "We shall never forget how precious your mother was."

"I find it difficult that my father just accepts all they do. As if he no longer cares about how things were."

"I know dear," Monika repeated solemnly.

"He always sides with Eileen when I say I want to keep anything," John's voice contained anger. "He says his first duty is now to Eileen and allows her to carry on with all her changing of things."

"Hello Monika," Eileen said deliberately loudly, as she came into the room.

"Hallo, Eileen," Monika responded neutrally.

Neither John nor Monika could be sure whether or not Eileen had overheard anything of their conversation. There was a strange tension in the room.

"Can I make you a cup of tea, Eileen?" John asked rising from his chair.

"No thank you, John," Eileen replied. "I must straightway go speak to the carpenter about the new floorboards. Good-bye for now," she said to

Monika and, frowning about something, busily left the room.

"Your mother taught you well," Monika praised John. "You sounded well-mannered then. Rosemary would be proud."

For John's sake and for Eric's, Monika attempted to conceal her dislike and mistrust of Eileen. "I must not," she demanded of herself, "say or reveal anything that makes it awkward for me to continue visiting John." But she was far from certain that her attempt was working. Eileen seemed always on edge when Monika visited John, and even more so whenever Monika engaged in conversation with Eric. Eileen was delicate about being a newcomer. Monika had known Eric since early childhood which was a decade longer even than she had known Rosemary. And Eric in marrying Rosemary, had married one of Monika's closest friends. There was a long history and much in common so that conversation between Monika and the Carpenter family came easily. All this went to make Eileen feel insecure.

"I guess," Monika told herself, "Eileen knows that I can see through her. She finds it repugnant that I know what she is about. And that I know all about the family."

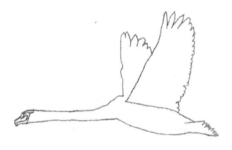

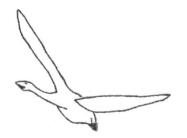

"John, how are you getting along with Eileen?" Monika returned to the subject a fortnight later when John seemed desolate and solitary.

"Rather poorly," he answered.

"Are you able to talk to her," Monika persevered, "much?"

"There were, and probably still are, good reasons for trying to be sociable," John broadened out. "Not only is Eileen now the lady of the house with whom we must live ......she is also....... somewhat incredibly....... my father's wife...... so it seems only fair to make an effort.......But when I try to share thoughts with her she just makes me feel like an alien. My words seem..... futile and misdirected. So......... I have more or less stopped trying," he admitted.

"Don't give up!" Monika urged.

"Well……..I suppose it must be obvious," John's voice fell, "that I cannot accept her. Anyhow, whatever the cause, we walk over one-another's graves. I sometimes literally shudder when I think of her. And she doesn't like young people much, I think."

"I must say, my boy," Monika spoke with a furrowed brow, "Life has forced you quickly to exchange youth for maturity. Eileen is *not* your mother. No-one will be able to listen and laugh with you as Rosemary did."

"I think Eileen can't wait for the day I leave home," John mused. "Whatever my needs are, they seem always to be the opposite of her needs."

"She is a hard person," Monika agreed. I too find that she regards normal conversation as a waste of time."

"Perhaps Eileen doesn't have any conversation at all?" John said. "Perhaps all she can think about is power. And about how to better her position"

"Oh, she has conversation enough when she needs it," Monika said grimly.

"It often seems," John meditated, "that her listening is confined to one purpose and one purpose only and that is to gather information about other peoples' circumstances. Sometimes she seems to be deliberately gathering information that she might use against *me*. But actually, in her scale of things, I am probably not important enough for that. Unless it is something to do with the house. But it is definitely information about others that she craves. And it is never your normal old gossips' information. She is above *that*, I grant her as much. No. What interests her is anything that has something to do with anyone's personal finances or business plans or investments."

"Yes," Monika concurred. "She never *gives* of herself, never speaks her heart. But! She *does* speak her mind. And goodness! Does she have a mind to chide and a mind to direct! Many in the village have felt it."

"Everyone that she doesn't need she considers a minion," John confirmed with unenthusiastic certainty. "She shuts down my spontaneity. If I try humour, she gives minimal responses and withdraws. Perhaps she just doesn't want to know. She is cold and distant, maintains an informed silence. I have come to expect nothing from her. *Nothing.*"

"Hmmmmm……." Monika said.

"She and my father often argue about money," John said. "One of their repetitive rows is about how and why she put the money from the sale of her house next door into her own bank account and did not share any of it with him."

There was silence for a few moments while each contemplated the matter.

"And what about your father?" Monika asked. "How is he……. within himself?"

"He said something yesterday about my bedroom being needed for other purposes."

"What other purposes?" Monika asked.

"I don't really know. Something to do with Eileen's son. I did question it but Eileen called him away to discuss something else so that we never finished the conversation."

"Hmmm…….." Monika said, "Well…….. perhaps you should try to find out more?"

"Yes," John agreed, "I should. But I wonder whether it will make any difference. My father has switched all his loyalty to his new family. Although it hasn't made him happy. The rows with Eileen are terribly loud, you know. I sometimes think all of Wimbledon must be able to hear them. Before mother died I thought Eileen's house was unwelcoming. Now I think ours is. My mother's presence has gone out of it. A hard-driving Jewish form has replaced our tranquillity."

The commandeering of John's bedroom occurred one morning while John was at school. He returned home in the late afternoon to a fait accompli.

Going as usual to his bedroom, he came to a halt at the doorway, gaping in disbelief.

His room was completely different. His things were not there. His bed, his cupboards, his bookshelves, his chair, the pictures on the wall, everything that Rosemary had carefully assembled for him over the years, everything except his big desk, all were gone. Instead, thoroughly cleaned and vapidly geometric, all of Neill Green's furniture and belongings had replaced his own. A new carpet perfectly fitted into smooth position gave off its smell of newness.

Completely unschooled in domestic combat, John made his way to the lounge where he could hear Eric and Eileen discussing finances.

"My room?" he stormed, interrupting angrily and without preface.

The newlyweds reacted with instant ire to this challenge.

"What do you mean?" Eric asked rising swiftly from his seat to meet the confrontation of his first-born. He was obviously prepared for conflict and extremely irritable at having to be prepared.

"Where are all my things?" John demanded.

"My Neill needs the space for his studies." Eileen retorted venomously.

"Is that so?" John shouted and stared at Eileen. "Well *I* need my room for *my* studies. "It is *my* room. It has been *my* room since the day I was born. I want it back and I want it back *now*."

He ran from them back to his room and began overturning new furniture, throwing things at the wall and doing as much damage as he could.

In response to the commotion, Eric and Neill Green and Neil Carpenter ran in. They overpowered John. In less than a minute Eric held John in an arm-lock on the floor. The step-brothers, Neil Carpenter and Neill Green, their work done, stood back but remained on alert. Side by side they looked on.

"The boy is very rude and has led too sheltered a life," Eileen raged. She had quickly followed the others to the disputed room. She looked from Eric and John to the two Neills and back again.

"Now that mum is dead," John, from his pinioned position on the carpet, raised his head to upbraid his father, "you care only about this new woman and her son. You have forgotten your first wife and your real family."

"Remember that you are just a child," Eric responded.

"But am I still *your* child?" John spluttered. "Since this woman came into our house, you have given every laudation to her son and forgotten that you already have two sons."

A brutal expression passed across Neil Carpenter's face. He clenched his fist, took a step forward, thought better of it, and took a step back again.

Still on the floor, John scowled up at his blood brother in contempt and disbelief.

"Marrying so soon after mum died," John continued with very little pause, "and," he nodded at Eileen, "bringing this woman to sleep in my mother's bedroom, it's disloyal. It's disgusting. My wrong-doings are peccadilloes by comparison."

"What are peccadilloes?" Neil Carpenter asked.

"You are offensive and insubordinate," Eric was incandescent. "As I have mentioned before," he insisted, "except you were not listening, Neill needs the big desk as a surface on which to roll out his engineering drawings. And your room is the only room large enough to accommodate his desk. That was the only reason for the exchange of rooms." Eric still pinned John to the ground but even as he did so he recalled all too clearly several critical comments directed at him of late. Not least of these concerned his choice of second wife and the transfer of attention from his old to his new family. Holding his son down, Eric wavered between attempting a reasoned approach and continuing his combative stance.

"I am just an expendable middle son now, aren't I father? No longer your first-born? Or only technically so? Now that you have a new family?" John spoke up bitterly from his place on the new carpet.

"Of course you aren't," Eric said releasing his son and standing back. The two Neills stepped up their readiness for a renewal of trouble.

"Goodness, you have a perfectly good room all to yourself," Eileen put in, her voice going up an octave in her version of reasoning. "Many a child in London would count itself very lucky to have what you have. Why can't you try to get on with my son in just the same way as your brother does?"

"Itself!" John echoed icily. "From a room with a view to the box room!" he added, picking himself up and making a show of vigorously dusting himself off as he did so although there had not been even one speck of dust on the new carpet. "Nice carpet," he said sarcastically.

"But," John continued, vehemently addressing Eileen, "the stupefyingly outrageous thing about this is that your son isn't even going to *be* here to use this room most of the time. Because he is going to be away at Oxford. So his room, which is really *my* room, is going to be *empty* for long periods."

"Yes," Eileen replied, "but for those times when he is home, my son's time is more important than yours. He is more advanced, more senior."

"Is that so," John looked at Eileen with disgust and contempt.

He looked at his father. "And you, father, will you not change your mind about your stepson's claim being more valid than your son's?"

He waited for a moment.

"Your silence tells me you find my question unanswerable. Perhaps you are afraid of your new wife?"

There being still no response from anyone present, John walked out.

He went to the small room he had now been allotted. There was barely space to squeeze around the edge of the bed. For a long while he sat on the end of the bed resting his chin on his palms. His mind drifted to other thoughts. Somehow it refused to focus on his predicament.

Unsure, until this moment, what name to use when speaking to Eileen, the incident brought another clarity to the youth's mind. To the curiosity of friends and associates and to the discomfort of both Eric and Eileen, John began from that moment on, emphatically and with excessive politeness, to address Eileen as "Mrs Carpenter."

Neill Green he simply ignored wherever possible.

"Perhaps he will come round in his own time," Eric suggested a week later to Eileen as John left the table after a particularly oppressive evening meal.

But John overheard his father. He turned in the doorway. "You two are completely self-engrossed," he said angrily and made to leave quickly before they could respond.

"You come back here!" Eric roared, incensed at yet another challenge to his authority.

John dragged himself back into the dining room and stood facing his father. Eileen, her mouth working in a perpetual chewing motion, glared angrily through her large smeared lenses at the slight figure before them, drawn up at semi-formal attention.

"You had better apologise to Eileen and to me young man, or there will be hell to pay." Eric's voice was curtly disciplinarian but not brutish.

"But don't you see, father?" John replied. "Hell has already been paid. Even *you* wouldn't want Hell to be paid twice, would you? This was once my mother's house. Now it is Mrs Carpenter's." The pathos in these words caused Eric to contain his Victorian apoplexy. One of Eileen's feet began to swing furiously backwards and forwards. It rocked her whole body so that her head nodded slightly. Eric suffered insufferable pressure. He was caught in the crossfire of his son's accusation of immoral haste and his new wife's demand that he quash the rebellion of her new stepson. But also, being the man of the house, he must contend with his own rage at being challenged where he had been always unquestionably paramount. He proceeded carefully. One thing was certain. He was out of his depth. He searched in Edwardian taciturnity for an appropriate target other than himself, against which to discharge his futile frustrations.

"The nub of the matter has to do with sensitivity and insensitivity" Eric said thinking out loud but also suspecting all the while that it might be better to downplay such sentiments, if not to scoff at them. Eileen, he knew, was not disposed to be lenient.

"If he can't like us, he will jolly well have to lump us," Eileen said fiercely to Eric, deliberately not troubling to lower her voice.

"Oh well," John said, looking directly at his father, "I'll leave you now, if you don't mind," he paused, "with your new happiness." And then, once more he turned and left the room but this time his departure went unchallenged.

Eric stared straight ahead for a moment before turning to Eileen. "It's only a matter of time before he goes off into the world on his own," he said to his new wife. "And then things will be smoother."

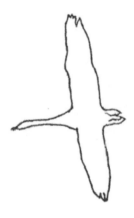

John's instinctive refuge was Monika's house.

"You see, John, my friend," Monika said when he described the latest incident, "Eric and Eileen are now so consumed by power struggles within their marriage that they can have very little spare energy and thought for your life and needs."

"Oh I *am* glad you also think that" John said with relief. "Sometimes I wonder whether it is me that is in the wrong. But you have more experience than me, and an arms-length view."

"Also remember, my boy, when you are troubled by the way they are, that love is often exclusive," Monika commented. "Some people are incapable of looking beyond their own togetherness. Much."

Monika's house quickly evolved from refuge to retreat and then to haven and then, almost without his being aware of it, became John's real home. He visited several times every week. They were beyond the formality of knocking on the door. Monika gave him a key so that he could let himself in at any time. His presence was natural. Often, as the spring advanced, he would arrive in twilit dawn only to leave after dusk.

"Our days are never long enough," she said. "Maybe I should stay over tonight?" he said. "I will bring you elder-flower water," she said. "To the table in the garden. I'll just change quickly." "But I love you in your dressing gown," he requested. She took a nervous half-step back and drew her gown more closely about her. "Would you like anything to eat?" she asked. "Your gown shimmers when you move," he said. "I have primroses, hyacinths and poppy seeds to go out," she said. "Toast and butter," he said. "It's still a bit cool for a gown in the garden," she said. "I like looking at you," he said.

"Besides the neighbours might see. And then you can mow the lawn and freshen up the flower beds while I go shopping," she evaded. "They won't see into the orchard," he said. "And what would you like for supper?" she asked. "I don't mind. Whatever you feel like making," he said. "You are so good with food. And with everything. May we have supper in the orchard again if it stays fine? And then read to one another again? It was so immaculate there in the quiet last evening. Let's start by learning another verse of 'The Rubaiyat' off by heart, then try 'Klingsor's Last Summer' or continue with 'Trekking On' and then, after that, see if we can still remember that verse we learned the day before yesterday. Isn't there a lot to read?" he asked." "Our reading is a special richness," she said. "A deep happiness. It's unusual. Our reading. It really is. Our souls meet when we read aloud to each other."

"You're still wearing your gown," he said when she appeared with the beaker of elder-flower water. "The sunlight makes it even lovelier, a little more transparent." She apparently ignored him but their eyes met in brilliant grey. "Only not quite transparent enough." She drew her chair to a secluded spot. "Bring the chair and table here behind the tree," she said. "It's more private." "I am glad you didn't change," he said. She did not really ignore him. He followed her with the table and then returned for his chair. "The gardening has always been my favourite task in this place," she said. "The coolth makes you prettily pointy," he said. "But this spring," she said, "our working and reading, eating and drinking, just living, has brought delight into the light." "I love it all," he said, "when we dig and weed and prune and build compost heaps and stop for picnic lunches on the lawn and look at insects and worms and give the flower-beds clean-cut edges." "We have come to *know* this piece of land," she said, "Our labour transforms it. It absorbs us and we absorb it." "I watch your body move while you work," he said. "And sometimes that is enough. Just to watch you. Bent over a flower bed. Or paused in a thought." "Some of the work," she said, "is physically pure. It has made us think creative thoughts. London's soil is *so* fertile." "A small piece of land," he said, "produces much. We never speak of love but our garden is our medium, our fertility."

"Yes," she nodded. "I feel it all. Just as you say. We are the lovers who must not speak of love………. never touch………." They sipped elder-flower water for a while. "Now," she said, "I am going to change before I bring out the breakfast. You've done quite enough looking for one morning."

"No I haven't," he said plaintively.

But Monika retreated. She went in. Soon she returned in gardening clothes with trowels and seed packets. Then she went back for the breakfast tray.

John acknowledged the status quo. And pondered it. He was old enough to begin to see into Monika's predicament. But not old enough to relinquish hope. "No-one need ever know," he told himself.

Sometimes, of a wet day, they would play chess. Or sit together for long periods on Monika's couch, reading or chatting or dozing. When she put her arm around his shoulder she told herself that the warmth in her heart arose out of simple mothering which, far more than softly approving, far more by far, Rosemary would definitely *require*. "If Rosemary is looking down on us," Monika questioned herself, "is there anywhere that she would draw a line? Would she mind? Or would she not mind? Is she beyond the cares of this world? Would she perhaps want me to go to the limit to teach her son many things as a means of safeguarding him against some of the terrible things of this world? I *am* after all her son's godmother, am I not? I could go even further than she could have gone. As a mother. She would have done all she could. As any mother would. Are John and I simply companions who bring comfort to one another? Perhaps there is a lot more that I should permit him? But what will that same old ever-present worldly world think? The world of gossip and scandal?"


The spring progressed. Monika struggled on with her indecision and her longing. As, in the pleasant shade of the orchard, they paused from their afternoon labour, cooling down with her lemonade, or in the morning, took a break from planting and tending, she did not reject the thoughts that arrived involuntarily in her mind, even though those same thoughts went on to take possession of her heart. The garden reflected their complexities, burgeoning and blossoming all around them. She tried for an intelligent overview. Neither did she banish John's advances nor did she submit. Deftly, with gossamer subtlety, steering a middle-course, she allowed no move. She understood men, did not dislike them for their intense and desperate needs. Indeed, she loved the need itself. Most especially she had patience for this youth.

"You are skilful and kind," John acknowledged their state of being. "It seems you know my inner thoughts and understand what is happening between us better than I do." He looked deeply at her. "I think you forgive me for the thoughts I have about you. And it is not only that you know and accept what is going on. You understand what you are doing far better than I do. You know how to respond."

"You must not worry," she said. "I am, as you observe, experienced. I like it that you like me. In fact I like it a lot. And I like you. A lot. And of course, it helps to be a woman and not to be in the first flush of desire."

Monika, however, secretly also acknowledged her own vulnerability. "My God," she thought, "I do not feel anywhere near as confident as I sound."

"And..................," Monika said one day. She often began conversations with the word, 'And' followed by a pause, especially when she had dwelt on a problem for several days. "And........ even had your father and Eileen not been completely taken up by their own disputes, they are, both of them, "too selfish and too proud." It is not just that they can think only of themselves and have little interest in your difficulties. It is also that Love is not an easy subject for them. I imagine they do not speak of love, not in any form, not of what exists between them, nor of the worlds of their children, nor of any such wondrous things within themselves or in the world without."

"They think discussion of love is 'theatrical' or 'histrionic,'" John agreed.

"I know that kind of marriage," Monika continued. "Everything in their personal lives is 'an arrangement' 'taken to be understood' or 'not to be harped on'. They much prefer to leave things unspoken. All nuances and subtleties, all the spires, domes and towers of the many cities of love, all its forests and numberless dales and canyons and deserts,......."

"Numberless dales and canyons!" John echoed.

".....canyons and deserts," Monika would not be interrupted, "its daring, its droughts and oases, all its countries and tribes and cultures and customs, all its harbours and havens, its flowers and thorns and colours, its romances and tragedies, all of that and much, much more are, so far as Eric and Eileen are concerned, relegated to the world of dangerous romantics and silly dreamers."

"Yes, I know," John responded slowly, searchingly. "To them poetry is sentimental guff and they silence any drift in the conversation from science to art. And in their case 'science' means 'money.' They seem to dread any thought or word which might reveal inner worlds or start uninvited conversation."

"Yes. They need to live in a practical, mechanical world," Monika asserted.

"My father," John said, "does sometimes, on Sunday afternoons, pick up a volume of George Meredith or delve into an essay. But he regards it all as heady stuff, a kind of semi-valuable profundity best left in obscurity. If it offers no mathematical proof, it is nothing more than light entertainment. When he puts the book down he sometimes says something like 'great wits are sure to madness near allied.' Last Sunday Eileen said to him, 'You're not reading that vapid nonsense again, are you?'"

"What sort of thing does Eileen read?" Monika asked.

"Oh, she doesn't really read," John said. "There are fewer and fewer interesting books on the shelves. She seems to study balance sheets and profit and loss accounts a great deal. And she is always pondering a clause in a lease or forecasting the gain or loss to be made on a foreign exchange transaction. So that's her 'reading'. In fact I don't think she would consider wasting time on anything else. To her, financial statements have real meaning. She likes to talk about the manipulation of statistics and is constantly on the look-out for clues about possible threats to her assets. She is dismissive of literature, even classical literature. Mind you, she definitely envies authors who grow wealthy from selling their books."


"Well..........," Monika said reflectively, "Eileen's single-mindedness and high opinion of herself seem to undermine everyone else's opinion of her. But........," she sighed, "most people are snobs about something. Aristocrats are too proud of their status. Liberals are snobbish about intellect. Even proletarians who say they hate snobs and the snobbish are snobs about their own idea of power. But Eric and Eileen must know," she paused, "that *big* consequences will flow from their decisions. It is just that," she concluded, "they cannot help themselves and *cannot* look about. They are actually *incapable* of grappling with their *real* problems. Those two *have* to be the ostriches they are and to work with subjects that will, as they see it, enhance their power. Their kind of power. They deny all else."

"It seems to me," John continued one day to Monika, "that I now have two step-parents. Even though one isn't. My father has diminished in stature, just like the view from my bedroom window has diminished. From the box room which is now mine I look onto the unbroken wall of Eileen's former house. It's a bleak contrast to what used to be. Do you remember the view I used to have before the step-brother took it over, leafy Wimbledon in summer and snowscape in winter?"

He nestled against Monika and she drew his arm around her shoulder. In his mind the soft warmth of her bosom against his chest, always most loveable, shimmered between phantasy and the maternal. "Dismal loneliness and isolated old age will be the result of all that is going on," Monika said looking out into an invisible distance. "Glad fulfilment will not be theirs."

"And………," John mimicked Monika's way of beginning an important thought with, 'And……...'
"And………., something else is happening," he said. "I may have lost the beautiful view from my old bedroom window. At home I may have lost many personal spaces, but here, here with you, day by day, I have something that grows closer and closer. Each day with you is more beautiful than the last. What we have is steadily overtaking that which is lost."

Monika nodded her agreement. But silently, to herself, she said, "Which………makes me tremble within and without."

At the house of Eric and Eileen the examination of post delivered by the postman became another source of friction. John regarded his step-mother's inquisitiveness about the contents of his mail as intrusive and offensive.

"Mrs Carpenter, do you always hold my mail up to the light, when it arrives?" John asked tersely when, once again, he caught Eileen in the act, "and study the handwriting and squint at the postmark?"

"It's the habit of a lifetime," Eileen replied, pricked once more into anger by what she regarded as John's insolence. "It is the result of having always been a responsible businesswoman. Does it bother you?"

"Do it for your own post," he said, "not for mine."

"I did not intentionally single out your letter," Eileen walked off aggrieved.

Whether or not it was a result of this incident, when an official looking letter arrived addressed to Mr John Carpenter, Eileen kept it for Eric instead of handing it to John. It was next to Eric's chair when he came to the table for the evening meal. Eric opened the letter and read it before handing it to Eileen, who in full view of John, also read it. As Eileen focussed on the content, she pushed back her chair and read it intently, her mouth working and a foot swinging swiftly back and forth all the while. It was only when, without a word, she passed the letter to John to read, that he realised the letter had been addressed to himself and was of a most confidential nature.

John stared at the letter heading. "Are you both blind?" he asked in intense anger. "Why are you reading my confidential mail? This is a letter from my doctor addressed to me about an intensely personal matter and it is *absolutely not* the business of either of you." He was beside himself with indignation. "Can you not *read*? Do you not see that the letter is headed up by the word 'CONFIDENTIAL' in capital letters. The capital letters are double underlined. *Double underlined*" he repeated very loudly." And now that I look, I see the word 'CONFIDENTIAL' is also in *large* capitals on the envelope. He looked in turn at Eileen, at John and at both the Neills who were present. "Do you not know the meaning of the word, 'CONFIDENTIAL?'"

"Everything that goes on under my roof is my business," Eric's eyes narrowed in reply.

"And you gave it to *her* to read," John said furiously.

The two Neills looked at one another and prepared for another confrontation.

"This letter," John waved the letter at Eric and Eileen, "is from my doctor. It is about my body, *very private* aspects of my body," John stressed, staring in intense disbelief at his father, "and *you* gave it to *her* to read! To *her* of *all* people. When you know she is *the last person* on this planet with whom I would discuss such a matter. You *know* that to me she is an enemy alien."

"Just as well it confirms there is nothing wrong with you then, is it not?" Eileen said hawkishly, looking at John, the beaded necklace attached to her spectacles moving in time to the swinging of her foot.

"This is not just some trespass." John said "It is the *rape* of privacy. Thank God, Mrs Carpenter, you will 'lead these graces to the grave and leave the world' only one 'copy'"

"What?" Eileen demanded.

Neill Green guffawed.

"Nothing," John answered. Still holding the letter, he walked out of the room without touching any food. No-one amongst those present thought it worth attempting to draw him back to the evening meal.

"My father might just perhaps, as my natural parent, have had some claim to the contents of that letter," John protested to Monika the next day when, in the privacy of her lounge, he described the latest quarrel. "But Eileen certainly did not."

"And yet you told me all about the whole worry even before you went to the doctor?" Monika said. It was only half a question. Partly it was a shared rumination.

"Yes, but you are my next of kin," there was not a split-second delay in John's reply. "Nowadays those two both rank only as step-parents. There is less and less that I can speak to them about. In contrast, I could tell you anything, *absolutely* anything, physical, philosophical or poetic, and be completely unembarrassed. Thanks be to God, whoever *He* is."

Monika nestled into him. "I am glad you feel that way about me," she said. "Very glad. But," she advised gently and seriously, "you need to detach from such anger about them."

"More than detach," John asserted. "I need to leave, go away, get as far from Wimbledon as possible." But he snuggled closer to Monika, absorbing her warmth, and in so doing missed the glimmer of pain that flitted across her face. She held him close and stroked his hair while she sought some distraction.

"Would you like," she asked, still holding him close, "to go to London with me one day soon to see "This Year of Grace?" It's on at The Pavilion."

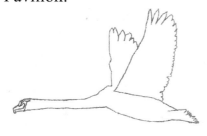

Further disputes arose. There seemed no end to the growing list of domestic disagreements in the Carpenter family. Yet the two Neills seemed largely unaffected. Even though their young lives took them along diverging paths they still occasionally found ways to continue the friendship begun in schooldays. Sharing an interest in flying they went to aircraft exhibitions and discussed Handley Page. Sometimes they visited airfields to study more closely the aircraft that now frequented London's skies.

One day Neil Carpenter, too, was caught up in Eileen's re-ordering of the house. He found himself moved out of his bedroom when it was taken over by Eileen as her office and library. His bed was placed in what was little more than a pantry adjoining the kitchen. "Aren't you angry about being expelled from your room?" John asked, surprised that his younger brother accepted so much without complaint or comment.

"It doesn't really bother me," Neil Carpenter replied. "If the old man wants his piece of fluff then he must accept her ways."

John stared in amazement at this statement. "We have never really understood one another, you and I, have we?" he said. "But at least I now have a new insight into your thinking."

"He really *doesn't* seem to mind about his room," John said to Monika a few days later when he described his increasing estrangement from his brother.

"The strains of living affect people differently," Monika said levelly. "It is a very difficult time for you all. Neil has his own way of coping."

"I heard the housemaid," John confided, "telling Eileen that she needs to buy him yet more shirts because he has again been cutting them up, dying them different colours, and turning them into scaled-down replicas of the flags of different countries and of various steamship lines. I hope we are not all going mad. He spends a lot of time alone in his room, reading in semi-darkness. To be fair he also goes out with his friends sometimes. But I have noticed that like me he has taken to leaving the table as soon as possible at meal times."

"Oh, you Carpenters don't know how lucky you are. You know nothing of real hardship," Eileen protested when John asked Eric if he thought Neil Carpenter was insecure. "If you knew what it was like to really suffer, you wouldn't complain so much."

John let the matter drop. But he stored away in his mind a question concerning what the 'real hardship', to which Eileen referred, might be. Or have been. And whether she herself might perhaps have been through a time in which she knew what it was to 'really suffer.'

Eric thought it best to accept Monika's suggestion that he visit her with John to discuss matters. "After all Monika and I have known one-another most of our lives," he admitted to himself.

At the meeting John was forthright. "My assessment of my step-mother" he said to Eric and Monika, "is that she relishes nothing like she relishes financial manipulation. She draws prestige from giving the financial commands which cut down her competitors or enhance her allies. She sees herself as a grand dame who controls underlings. Her only really humane instinct is to protect and promote Neill Green. Nothing in the universe, other than money and power, deserve more than a passing glance from *Mrs Eileen Carpenter*." John was seated alongside Monika on her couch. Eric had instinctively taken the chair that, during her lifetime, Rosemary had always used when she visited. "I mean to say," John continued, "do these women who take on the role of step-mothers even begin to think what they do when they marry into an existing family?"

"So............, John," Monika said glancing at Eric and then taking John's hand and looking into his face as she spoke, "many men find life just *too* lonely without a woman. I know there have been harmful disputes in your family but I think we should acknowledge that your father has always provided for you. You have never known hunger and there has always been a roof over your head."

"He seems to be completely unable to see beyond his own needs," John answered.

Eric remained silent.

"Your father, like most men," Monika continued, "*needs* to be seen as the head of his house. Your mother was very good at playing to his strengths and harnessing them for the good of you all. Rosemary was also very good at being uncomplaining. Too good, as it turned out in the end." She brushed away a tear. "If only she had thought of *herself* a bit more and sought medical assistance *sooner*."

"But now," she turned to Eric, "since Rosemary died, that essential understanding which was her gift to you and to the boys, *and* to us *all*, her role in the family happiness, has been lost. You need to think, Eric, that not only are John and Neil *your own sons*, but to remember that Rosemary was their mother. You now have to keep *those* thoughts alive as well as giving Eileen the attention she deserves."

"Do you think Monika," John asked, "that my father's mother ever *even attempted* to teach him to consider others? Because if she failed in that, then *she* may be partly to blame for bringing our family crashing down."

Eric sat back with a constrained frown and regarded his son critically but still said nothing.

"No, John," Monika gently remonstrated, "that is just *too* hard. Your father is also a human-being. And no mother can guarantee the decisions of her child. We cannot know what thoughts your grandmother had or what difficulties may have distracted her during her life-time. Remember that I knew her when I was a little girl. I always thought she was a good, if rather silent woman. It is hard enough to understand the living without trying to reach back into the minds of those who have been long dead."

When Eric rose to leave, Monika accompanied him to the door. They left John sitting in the lounge.

"*Eric*," Monika spoke with natural strength, "we knew each other a little too well long before we knew Rosemary. And you know that nowadays John spends a lot of time with me. I am very *glad* to know him well. I want to help by giving him other things to think about, perhaps even to widen his education. That is what Rosemary made me promise I would do. And I promised her *gladly* and in the tenderness of her extremity. And so I plan to take him out to London from time to time. Because you and Eileen do not seem to have time for such diversions. Does any aspect of my association with John bother you in any way?"

Eric glanced deeply into her eyes. "No, not at all," he said after only a momentary hesitation. "Jolly good thing! Very good idea! Rather than it being a bother, I give you my thanks. I am glad of it. Couldn't be better. It's a weight off my mind. Thank you," he said, clasping her hand with both his hands. They looked at one another for a long moment, remembering a shared childhood.

"Good," Eric repeated and left without another word.

"But mother!" Neill Green had said when his mother, Eileen, first told him of her plan to marry Eric Carpenter, "if you marry, how will we stay in control of what we have?"

"Do you doubt my forethought son?" Eileen countered. "Of course there will be, already is, an antenuptial contract in place. I was not born yesterday, you know. We live in the twentieth century. I will control the combined finances *in the same way* that I control the existing finances."

"With an iron hand?" Neill Green asked.

"Of course, son," Eileen affirmed, "with an iron hand. Eric has put his signature to a contract by which he will forfeit this house and half of his investments if he exits the union. It wasn't too difficult to drive the bargain. Eric is not financially sophisticated. If I had not acquired this power I would not have entered into the marriage. As simple as that. Of course he would keep his children. If he accepts my ways he can look forward to an affluent old age. I will at least manage that for him. It will cost comparatively little to have servants tend him when he is elderly. I arranged it all in such a way that he thinks of me as his house-keeper and his insurance."

"And by the way, at the time of signing the antenuptial contract, we also signed our new irrevocable back-to-back wills. If I die before Eric you will have ninety per cent of the entire Carpenter net worth. Of course, if I die after Eric you will have it all."

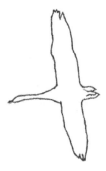

"Eric is largely oblivious to his own shortcomings," Monika explained to John the next day. "But he is not alone in that. Many of us cannot see our own faults. If we could, there would be fewer of them. However, I believe that in the last few months various quite important people have told your father to his face that things are not right. He appears not to hear. Because if he did hear he would alter his behaviour. But……….. apparently……… he takes no steps to change anything. His belief has always been that the decision of the man of the family, right or wrong, must be final and absolute. We have all always known that about him. All of us have known it. He was like that when he and I were children. I accepted it then because I was so much younger than him. Perhaps I am still inclined to accept it even now. Circumspectly.                       It's just………………easier."


"He was definitely the head of the house when mother was alive," John lamented, "but now I suspect his attempt to retain that status is all mere posturing because he is *so* pushed around by Eileen. Nowadays he is not head of anything! Seems to spend his time just bumbling around. Everything feels so different now from how it was with mother. She never spoke to him the way Eileen does, never screamed at him. They were happier. It all just makes me want to move away from home and find some way of belonging. I long to fit in, to belong once more, whether it is to a woman or an organisation. Or even to a group of friends."


"I saw how your mother made your father happier," Monika lingered over the thought. "Happier than he was as a child. And happier than he is now. Happiness was your mother's gift to your father. Paradoxically," she mused, "Eric can engage in charming, free-thinking intellectual conversations. I have, with Rosemary and others, been party to them. And enjoyed them. His thoughts and words engender great respect amongst friends and acquaintances. But unfortunately his liberal generosity vanishes at any threat to his own comfort or any real scrutiny of his strongly held opinions. But," Monika checked herself and frowned, "I must be careful not to criticise. Just like Eric, we all have ideals and just like him we all sometimes struggle to live up to them. I am no different from the next man or woman. Certainly no better."

"Many of the bonds between my father and I have been severed," John declared.

"I do often ponder possible solutions for the Carpenter predicament," Monika said slowly. "Often..... because your family means so much to me. Always has done. Having known you all for a lifetime....... There are various paths you might follow, John. But it is easier to think them than actually to put them into practise. So," she continued, "with regard to your thoughts about belonging, you could, as you say, 'choose to belong to a person or you might even choose to belong to an organisation.' But I think I know, John, what kind of organisation it is that you have a mind to join. *Fascist membership* holds real dangers and I do not want you falling foul of all *that*, my dearest." She stroked his hair and looked imploringly into his eyes as was her wont when she was concerned for his welfare. "I hope you aren't going to allow yourself to be swayed by the fashionable trends of our time....... Women....... And organisations. They both have the power to do more harm to you than good. Better just to be yourself. You have such a good brain, my boy. Your plain existence might, by itself, of its own endeavours bring greater reward than any 'belonging' or any 'membership.' Be independent. Be yourself. To the *full*. You have a big chunk of individuality which is itself a foundation. It is the key for being a success in your own right. Self-reliance is a way of life."

"Yes, well," there was aggrievement in John's voice, "my father and Eileen often talk about Neill Green's education and career. Almost never about mine or my brother's. They think work is the altar on which life should be sacrificed. As I disagree with their idea of work, it follows that I already think for myself. I do without parental guidance. Partly I am envious and partly I don't mind. Because I think there must be something *more*, something greater than the everyday working life to which, they take it for granted, I will dedicate my existence. Certainly I don't want their kind of devotion to money-making as my way of life."

John paused for a moment. "Mind you," he continued with a grin, "my brother is strangely oblivious to such matters. But then he wouldn't know a beatitude if he collided with one."

"You may no longer have your parents to consult," Monika said, "but you have me."

John's acknowledgment of this devotion was to furrow his brow for a moment. "So……………." he asked, "Why do you think that belonging to a woman or belonging to an organisation could hurt me?"

"Oh, my dear," Monika answered with serene certainty, "I fear mesalliance. Whether it be with a woman or with some Fascist organisation."

"I suppose you are right," John said, returning Monika's gaze, and trying to imagine the possibilities of the future.

There came a brief silence. Monika stirred slightly in her chair in a way that suggested some powerful thought troubled her.

"I need to talk to you about something," she said. "Something very important."

"Of course," he said, looking at her and wondering what was coming.

"Your mother is not here," Monika continued, a patient and serious note in her voice. "Normally it would be your mother's task to tell you certain things. *Eileen* is certainly not going to do it. Nor Eric. I know him. And so it has become my duty to speak to you. Because nowadays I am your next of kin. So would you accept it if I tell you a few important things?"

"Of course," John said again, an eyebrow raised.

"You are a young man," she said, and now a forthrightness and fearlessness was about her. "It would be perfectly natural that you long to undress a young woman. Am I right or am I wrong?" she asked.

Taken aback at first, John blushed and looked down. But then he looked straight at her. "You are right," he replied.

"Well now. Has anyone ever talked to you about any of the things that might happen or should happen or would be best for both of you to happen once you have undressed her?" she asked.

"The things you ask!" he said. And then, "No," he answered.

"So............," she said, "listen carefully to me now because I am going to offer you some fragments of an older woman's discerning."

If Monika hadn't been so well known to John, he might almost have misinterpreted the sound in her voice as scolding.

"For your own good and *especially* for your own protection, you need to learn some things I can teach you and to keep in your head a few vital details," she said. "And..............although the things I will tell you," she smiled and relaxed a little, "concern the physical operation of the body, they are closely linked to the soul and have a big effect on happiness. In short I want to teach you what I know about making the most of it all."

Monika took John on a verbal journey, describing where to find things and what to do with them and how to honour and when to be patient.

"Never be dismayed at yourself, my friend, for admiring a woman," she concluded. "Women are often very glad to be admired. But don't let your admiration be obvious. Get clever at keeping your assessments to yourself. Hide your longing. It is not to be harped on. Hide it from everyone, not just from the girl. Don't speak to your friends about it. Conceal it…….. *Until*, that is, you have been given what you seek. But. And this is important. Once a woman has given you access to her person, do not stint on subtle appreciation of her. Because, in the ubiquitous search for the highest heights, she will have entrusted *you* with her essence and chosen *you* as her companion. This is no small gift. In fact it is a very big gift indeed. Unfortunately, sooner or later, most lovers lose sight of this truth. They come to take it for granted. And by so doing lose one of the greatest things they ever knew. Just by allowing it to fall by the wayside. Subtle appreciation, which is a form of gratitude and recognition, will be acceptable. For the most part. And noticed not only by the lady but by all who know you. Noticed in unnoticeable ways. Noticed and welcomed. The ripples of security you create will spread wide.

Although................. come to think of it,......... there is a time for everything. For the loud as well as for the subtle...........

*Always* tend your love. *Never* neglect it. Even when you are *very* tired. Because neglect can bring *the most dire* consequences........

And.........when I think of all the lovely goings-on between men and women, I think of the words of William Blake. Do you know, can you guess, which words I might be thinking of?" she asked.

"No," John answered.

"Blake wrote," she smiled, "'The nakedness of women is the work of God.'"

"*But*," Monika became intent, once more, on her subject, and intensely serious, "when it comes to 'the nakedness of women' you have to be *most* careful, my boy, more careful, more constantly thoughtful and alert than you are about almost anything else. Do you know *why*?"

"Why?" John asked shyly.

"Because, and it is of *supreme* importance that you know this, and there are not any nuances about it......."

Monika went on to talk at great length and in considerable detail about the dangers of disease.

"So?" she asked after a while. "Have I made it *clear* to you? Have you taken on the *full* gravity of what I am telling you?"

"I think so," John replied glumly.

Monika laboured the point, "Think very hard about it, John. *Always* think about disease. Because...... if you are not constantly careful your love-making could make you very ill. It could bring disease that literally makes you mad. It could, in fact, even result in death. The moment, my boy, you "go in unto" any woman, as The Old Testament so poetically puts it, you really do risk *everything*. It really is, in the most profound sense, a matter of life and death, a matter of 'just one wrong move and you're dead'. *Just one wrong move.* It only takes a few seconds for the damage to be done. *Every* man and *every* woman is at risk in this way. *All the time.* And *all* through life it *shall always be* a risk. And now, today, my dearest, it is my duty to ram this harsh medical lesson into your beautiful, much beloved brain, and by so doing to defend your very life. Do you forgive me for telling you so much?"

"Of course I forgive you," he said.

"And don't forget, my friend, however much the church is right to demand monogamy of us, it is the nature of men to be curious about the nakedness of women. And therein lies the danger. For men are seldom satisfied with viewing just one woman. Men are naturally fascinated. All men. Although some resist. But men have an instinctive yearning to know about different women. All kinds of women. Biblically, this is called 'knowledge'. And not only knowledge of women's bodies but also of women's minds. All women are different and the fundamental individuality of each woman emits a magnetism that is designed by Nature to draw men in, to fascinate them. All this happens all the time. Even though some try to play down its importance by saying there is only one female form. By saying once you have seen one, you've seen them all."

"Well…….." John, having listened with an awe that grew into a terror, protested, "if men and women are that attractive to one another……… What are we supposed to do?"

Monika touched his knee. "There are *several* things you *can* do," she said, "several creative ways around the problem. There are ways to engage which will enable you to enjoy the company of women without endangering yourself. Or endangering the woman. And most women, I promise you, will," she said soothingly, "respect you for it. And there are ways to……. disengage…………. Would you like me to tell you about some of these ways?"

"Yes please," John answered.

After long discourse, Monika changed the subject.

"And we haven't yet even begun to discuss that other matter of which we spoke when first we mentioned these things this morning."

"Which matter?" John asked, feeling saturated with thoughts he must still digest.

"The possibility that you might enlist in or belong to some organisation as a means of diverting your mind from the present family difficulties," she said.

"But," Monika added thoughtfully, "we've done a lot of talking today. Let's spend the rest of the evening gardening. We can talk about that other belonging another day. I am going to finish those scones I was making. You take the chairs and the garden table and

go sit in the shade and read your book.
I'll bring out some scones in a while."

In the very early hours, birdsong beginning, first light spreading soundlessly through the still air, John arose from a restless bed. He found paper and pencil to write a poem.

# Nuances and Subtleties

for Monika

'Not to be harped on!'
And yet.
All the nuances and subtleties,
all the spires
domes and towers of the many cities of
love,
all loves' numberless forests
and dales,
canyons and deserts,
all the droughts, oases and firestorms
of love,
all the countries, tribes and maps,
the cultures, customs and expressions,
all love's harbours, havens, scents and
flowers,
the thorns, buds, colours and leaves,
all the romances and tragedies,
all the intrigues, all the graces,
from time immemorial, world without
end,
all the labyrinths of sight and mind,
love's embraces,
all and more are sweet Monika's.

Canon Richards in full regalia, black cassock and white collar, appeared at the door of The Carpenter house. He was a well-built man, strong, with perfect white hair. His massive sense of purpose made Wimbledon too small for him.

"Come in, sir," John said showing the clergyman into the lounge where his father was reading.

Canon Richards wasted no effort on pleasantries. "How are things going with your new family?" He glared at Eric and there was little attempt to conceal anger and distaste. With Rosemary's death he had lost not only a personal friend and a hard-working member of his church but a whole family from his congregation. "I think the new Mrs Carpenter is of the Jewish faith which is why your whole family has ceased attending The Anglican Church?" he asked.

"Perhaps," Eric replied in instant neutrality from his arm-chair.

John carried in a plate of biscuits. Canon Richards declined a proffered chair.

"Even if you have allowed your family to give up all religious observance of any kind, I hope you can see that your son, John, here," he indicated John with a smile and a wave of his arm, "is entangled in youth's web of growth and self-discovery. Unfortunately the change in his family circumstances means he is, to all intents and purposes, on his own. His growing-up is unaided. He must undertake the scrupulous study and metering of his young thoughts and attitudes alone. And at the same time extricate himself from the dreary mystery of a world grown cold. Grown cold at your instance."

"Extricate himself from a world grown cold?" Eric echoed the words but turned them into a question. "At my instance?" Being accustomed to active approval from Canon Richards, he now hastened to adjust to this reversal of attitude.

"Yes," Canon Richards continued, "you are pushing him into the age-old realms of the dispossessed. He is looking for ways to reconcile, to avenge and to replace. Who knows what may come of it?"

"How do you know this?" Eric asked.

John remained silent.

"It is common knowledge in the parish at present," Canon Richards replied.

The conversation faltered on for a minute or two and then Canon Richards left. There was an abrupt formality in the handshake and a searching gaze at Eric.

Monika listened carefully. "'Dispossessed' was a powerful word for Canon Richards to use," she said to John. "But perhaps it is the correct word. Although," she hesitated, "it is probably wrong to assume the worst. And yet. Perhaps in the circumstances it is not altogether wrong. I suppose a priest must keep a watchful eye on his flock."

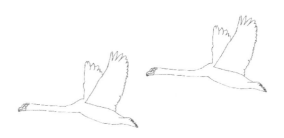

Eric's encounter with the family physician was even more negative.

"Blinking cheek!" Eric reported back to Eileen. "He told me that to the detriment of my natural children I am paying too much attention to my new wife. Does he forget that I have been paying his blinking substantial quack-fees for more than a decade? How dare he take me aside in a public place and be so forward. It is certainly not professional. And it's none of his blinking business anyway. Damn nerve! Who does he think he is? Upstart!"

"Oh, you must change physician! Immediately!" Eileen responded when they spoke about the reprimands. "We cannot have that! And as for the church. The church is just a racket."

John and Neil Carpenter were at the dining table. Household discipline required them to be punctual for the evening meal.

"Where's dad?" Neil asked.

"In the office talking with the lady of the house," John answered his brother by birth. "About money.......
Again……….. Dad and Eileen always insist to anyone who will listen that dad is free to think, free to work and to earn money, or not, as he pleases, but…………"

"And so he is, surely?" Neil Carpenter was quick to interrupt with a mixture of combativeness and querulousness, before John could continue his train of thought.

Eric, coming into the room overheard what had been said and how it had been said. "Eileen is my indispensable soulmate," he said to his sons, understanding at once the drift of their conversation. "She gives me a freedom to live and she keeps house for us all. She continues where your mother left off. That is all." He turned his palms downwards.

"That is *all*?" John repeated pointedly as Eileen came in with a bowl of vegetables.

"Yes, that is all," Neil echoed, his voice filled with unexpectedly intense aggression and contempt.

"You are clearly oblivious to our predicament," John said, eying his brother.

"And you are such a weed," Neil sneered at John.

"I see you are on the same subject again, John." Eileen's anger was instant. "Tell him to stop, Eric. We can't have him spoiling our lives. Tell him to stop now!"

"Can we have some sense?" Eric asked the question which was actually an order.

"The theme of the new Carpenter household," John continued undeterred, "is that you are paramount, Dad. But the theme is false. You promote the idea of your unfettered state but in fact real control is exercised by Mrs Carpenter."

"Oh, shut up!" Neil's retort held, once more, the threat of physical violence.

"The truth is," John continued, "that Mrs Carpenter outwits you and subsumes the Carpenter assets."

"Subsumes?" Neil mocked and goaded.

"Leave the table! Now!" Eric commanded his elder son.

"Surely it must be," John protested to Monika, "that Unconditional Love is unchangeable, just like The Deity from which it issued is unchangeable? Surely Unconditional Love is a form of The Deity? Even an actual part of The Deity? There must be certainty that death cannot harm it, mustn't there? Surely Unconditional Love continues in the ether after its viability on Earth has ended? Otherwise is The Deity not eternal."

"What has made you ask such powerful questions, my love?" Monika stood slightly back, looking at John. She reached out and touched his cheek.

"I heard them last night," John lowered his voice even though no-one else was present, "at it. The sound came through the ceiling from their bedroom to mine. It is just too awful to be woken at night from my sleep by the clamour of their intimacy. And it is going on in my mother's bedroom. In my mother's *bed*."

"On earth," Monika said, "everything is fleeting." She enfolded John in an embrace. "But we must *hope* that our best things live on somewhere in some perfect eternity. Otherwise our lives do all seem pretty purposeless."

The next day, after school, John went straight to Monika's house.

"As fate and timing would have it," he said thrusting a sheet of paper into Monika's hand, "the lesson in English literature today centred on Hamlet's mother, Gertrude."

Monika took the sheet of paper and read the words John had neatly copied onto the page.

> "Have you eyes?
> Could you on this fair mountain leave to feed,
> And batten on this moor? ha! have you eyes?
> You cannot call it love, for at your age
> The hey-day in the blood is tame, it's humble,
> And waits upon the judgement, and what judgement
> Would step from this to this?"

I know the passage," Monika said looking briefly at the page. She held her hand to her cheek in contemplation.

"It's exactly my situation, isn't it?" John demanded.

"Well, no," Monika said, forcing a calmness upon herself. "It's not the same as your situation. In your case no-one was murdered. And your circumstances, unfortunate as they are, are nowhere near as bad as Hamlet's."

John allowed her judgement. "I suppose you are right," he agreed, subdued.

"We must be wary of trying to turn literature into a weapon, my love," Monika continued. "The similarity you have with Hamlet is that your new family is disagreeable but that is about where the similarity ends."

"But wasn't Shakespeare himself using literature as a weapon?" John asked half rhetorically.

"No," Monika said. "I don't think so. Shakespeare was just embellishing a bit of history as a way of earning his living. He wanted to show the world as he saw it, not to take sides. He was adept at concealing what he actually believed partly because that was his temperament and partly because it was really dangerous, in those days, to do otherwise. An artist could not just say or write or paint as he wished. Good Queen Bess's secret police were watchful for anything that might imply a threat to the state. For his own safety Shakespeare needed to be very careful. So he presented everything in a way that was not only blameless but also, to make it interesting, *most* vivid. And..........by the way........., he may actually have felt more at home with the rich and educated than with the poor. It is probable that powerful Londoners at the time just about tolerated him because they saw him as almost one of theirs."

John contemplated this for a moment.

"But *you*.......you for your own good," Monika continued, "you must create a healthy way out of your adversity. And I am anxious to help you in any way that I can."

"I know you are," John said embracing her.

"I think," Monika suggested, "that sometimes, especially when you feel troubled, you should sit at your desk and write down your thoughts in great detail. It is a way of purging yourself of awful things you feel. And when you have written it all down and read it back to yourself, you should destroy what you have written, burn it, so that no-one else ever reads it."

"But I don't have a desk any more," he said.

"You can use mine," she said.

"And now," she said, happily and determinedly changing the subject, "as it is the end of the week, we are going out together. I am thinking of the train to Waterloo and then a ride on an open-top omnibus if it is still light. Or even if it isn't. And we can have supper somewhere nice in London. Come on."

John awoke again, in the early hours, to sounds of intimacy from the parental bedroom. He turned over and reached to the place on the floor next his bed where he had placed the note-book and pencil bought at Monika's suggestion. On the front cover of the book, he had written, "MY TABLES."

Opening the note-book to its first page, he began to write.

Firstly he wrote,

## "PREFACE"

"It is meet that I set it down in my tables."

And then he wrote a heading.

# "UNCONDITIONAL LOVE."

He underlined the heading.

"Profanities," he wrote, "occur in the world of man. They attack many things including Unconditional Love. And so Unconditional Love is not immortal. It can be harmed, foreshortened or fade. Unconditional Love can be crippled by spite. All manner of things can end it. It can occur in any person, good or bad. It does not have to die when the lovers die. But if and when it occurs, then it is a gift that must be nurtured in death as in life. It is often not obvious to the receiver or even to the giver or to the world at large that it has been given and received. It is the highest love, supreme above all the many other loves. In a lifetime it is usual that the instances of Unconditional love may be easily numbered on one hand."

These words flowed readily once he had begun writing.

"But," he continued with a new paragraph, "maybe all that is just Love. For it is truly inconceivable that Unconditional Love can die."

John turned a page and set down a new heading.

'PATERNAL MATTERS.'

This too he immediately underlined. He paused for quite a few moments. And then began writing again, very fast.

"The daily disbelief," he wrote, "that he would countenance such faithless changes, be so blind to continuous carpet-bagging, continues to expand.

And yet. I must admit that when a man's wife dies, he has a right, more than a right, a duty, to be happy. But what weakness would drive a man to remarry? Is it fear of loneliness?"

"There are women in every society, always have been, specially designed by Nature to fill this vacuum. Once a man has experienced Unconditional Love, there is no need for further marriage. Women of the night, who are also women of the day, are there to fill the void, supply the need, be the complete solution."

"And should not," John continued to write, "the man's children have some redress if their step-mother engages not in mere pilfer, but in deliberate acquisition of the entire estate that would have been theirs, had their mother not died? Some would call the step-mother's activity theft although the law would not call it that. Is not such a step-mother's activity worse than prostitution? Is it not a grand prostitution sanctioned by the law? Real prostitutes save families by being a diversion. They charge an agreed fee. There is a short-term contract and the contract ends. For this good work the law imprisons them. By contrast, step-mothers are there for ever. They destroy families. Their monetary fee is the total monetary value of the man and his family. And that is only their monetary fee. They also take control of other kinds of assets, things we might think of as non-monetary assets. And they continue in this position of power even if the marriage they have entered becomes deeply unhappy! The evil done by step-mothers afflicts succeeding generations. Amongst the laws many failures is its inability to address emotions. What is the value of the law? Who, really, makes the law? Is family law really only a means of saving the church and state money and effort? It seems the law is made by the cunning and the slothful. It works for the experienced and the strong against the innocent. And if the husband connives at the plundering of the estate, what then of the law?"

So.............

"Blessed are the poor"?

John paused. Then he turned another page and wrote a new heading. This too, he underlined in a deliberate manner.

## <u>"DESECRATION AND RECONSECRATION."</u>

"It falls to me to keep alive that which is more valuable than time. Memory."

"I have been writing down some thoughts," John showed his notebook to Monika. Like Hamlet I have called this book 'MY TABLES'. May I keep it in a drawer in your desk?"

"You do understand, John, don't you" Eric said in a conciliatory way one peaceful evening, "that Eileen and I keep a fond and respectful memory of your mother?"

"But!" John was aghast, "you left no part of her house as it was when she died. No tiny shrine. You have altered every single corner of it."

"That we move with the times does not mean we do not mourn," Eric answered.

"Always think young, John," Eileen put in.

"I must not forget the past," John answered. "Good night," he said and left. And as he walked to his room he thought, "Hollow, all hollow, worse than hollow. Step-families. Duplicitous sophisticates who have sacrificed and forgotten the simplicity of plain truth in their attempts to convince themselves. They cast about anywhere rather than look within. There is no straight-forwardness because that would reveal too much. Even to themselves. They want things their own way and they do not want to feel guilt. Most especially they abhor any suggestion that the world might think them other than innocent. A skin of moral certainty must encase their cesspool."

"That was a hard match," Monika said as they drew breath after a summer evening of tennis.

"Oh, you're better than me," John said.

And then, "Monika?" he asked, sipping her home-made lemonade, watching her towel away her perspiration, "do thoughts ever come unbidden into your head that you really, really, really did not intend to think? Such thoughts that you think, 'But, I am not to *think* these thoughts, where do they come from and how do I make them stop coming?'"

"Yes dear," Monika replied, "I think it happens to most people. My reverie I will never silence. But in silence lies my peace of mind. Why? What have you been thinking?" She leant forward to brush away an ant. John noticed that she looked, despite her years, agonisingly pretty in her midi-pleated tennis dress with its Art Deco embellishments. The exertions of their match had given her high colour. He tried not to gaze at her feminine form. But failed. She was very fit. The breathlessness which had caused her bosom to rise and fall was now quickly subsided. The pretty feet in their white socks and tennis shoes were neatly side by side. She was most finely built. And fully attentive to him.

"Well," he said, "there have been so many changes in daily life that I find my view of myself to have been…….. profoundly changed in an unexpected way."

"What is the profound change?" she asked, interested and perfectly at ease in his company.

"I think I …….. ," he caught his breath and swallowed, "I think ……I…..," his voice shook, "I love you," he disclosed in a kind of terror.

Her eyes fixed on his for a long moment. She reached out and settled her hand on his knee. Then she put her head back and laughed a loud, long, comradely laugh so that he saw into her mouth behind her rows of teeth. "Well, I should be very sad indeed if I thought you didn't," she said inching closer and stroking his hair. "The more so as half the village also thinks you do."

"What?" John gasped.

"Yes," she continued. "Our situation is obvious. But do not worry on that account. It is clear to all who know us, to anyone that looks, that I am the stand-in for your mother....... The man I wanted died on The Somme and all my friends know it. I reconciled myself years ago to the fact that The Great War had so decimated the men of my generation that I would be unlikely to marry. I try to find happiness in other ways. I play tennis. I admire Helen Wills. I grow flowers. I

go to the theatre and the picture-house.
I go to restaurants and tea-rooms. I am
independent." She thought for a
moment. "Of the love between thee
and me," she continued, "I shall not
say much. But you may take comfort. I
love you too. And of it I think neither
of us should speak. Because powerful
as words may be, for what we have
they are just plain inadequate. Silence
is better. Much better. Very unusually.
For what we have."

Days passed.

They were in the orchard again, lying side by side on the blanket. In perfect peace. It was evening.

"I think we should give your house a name," he said. "We should call it 'Clear Sky'. Because here we found loveliness."

"Okay," Monika agreed. "We shall call it 'Clear Sky' and the name will always remind me of you. Long after you have gone."

"Gone?" John was startled. "I am not going anywhere."

"No. Not now, you aren't. But one day you will. A young girl will come and take you away from me and I will yield because that will only be right."

"It's going to take a great deal for any woman to separate me from you," he said. "A whole bevvy of nubile maidens couldn't do it."

"It helps," she said, "when you look back, to know you did your best."

"It's your eighteenth birthday soon," Monika said. "Would you like to invite a friend or three to dinner?"

"I would love dinner," John replied, "but just you and I. My friends are rough and too immature for your house. I've already told my father I will be out that day. And night."

"Your mother always thought of you as a 'home-bird'," Monika said, "but I notice you have been going out more...... and staying out...... which worries me a bit. Of course I am glad to see you growing strong and independent. And....... it is a comfort to me that I have heard a warmth of friendship in your conversations with your friends."

"Going out more?" John echoed.

"Yes, going out more," Monika repeated, slow to expand, leaning languidly against a door-frame and examining him with a love-light in her eyes.

"Oh, you are always so careful not to be provocative," John said, seeing once more not only the aspect of feminine beauty she presented, but also the full value of the friendship she offered. He no longer found it necessary to conceal his gaze and admired her intently. "And it seems to me that *you* have so many friends because you are free and ingenuous."

"Many acquaintances and a *few* good friends," she said honestly.

"Perhaps they are, in your case, almost the same thing?" he suggested. "But, to answer your question," he added, "I *have* been going out more. You are right about that. It is a way of avoiding the step-family in the evenings. Those evenings when I'm not with you. Being only a remote moon in their solar system they seldom comment on my absence. Perhaps they don't even notice. They are not *kind* like you, Monika. And so I am just glad to get away from them and all their bickering. I am sorry, by the way, that I wasn't here on Tuesday."

"Did you go anywhere nice?" she asked. "I was expecting you."

"Well........, I was continuing my *search*," he said. "That search we have sometimes discussed, the search for...........a way of life.............. Do you remember that notice board we looked at?" he asked.

"The one at the library we laughed at because among the notices of meetings concerning everything from art exhibitions to town planning someone had popped in a naughty advertisement?" she smiled.

"Yes, exactly." He faltered. "Well............I didn't go to the talk about 'New Uses For Electricity.' But I did go to the political meeting you didn't want me to attend."

"Ah....... And? .... What did you learn?"

"It was as you said it would be," John answered. "Stormy and thuggish. Bucket-loads of wind. On several occasions the debate did actually give way to fisticuffs. Actual *blood* was spilled! People became heated over the matter of the French occupation of The Ruhr in 1923 and the collapse of the mark. I found myself contending with the intense thrill of the debate and the simultaneous need for inner calm. The intended subject was the danger that the injustices of the Versailles treaty may cause yet another war. But it all deviated into an argument about why The Great War started in the first place."

"Oh," Monika said pensively, "If the German airships return to drop bombs on us once more, I shall fully understand the reason. And…………..But yet……. I want *no part in all that madness*. There is not a *single* violent fibre in my body. So I hope and pray that you will forget about all this political stuff, my boy, and not go to any more political events. But…….. keep in mind that whatever you decide, no matter what you do, I shall still love you. And that most dearly, young man."

"And for that I shall always be thankful," he replied. "So much in this life is about the included, the excluded and the discarded………

But, *honestly*!…………" John continued, "The British, French and Americans could *not* have thought of a better way than The Treaty of Versailles of starting another Great War. Even if they had *deliberately* set out to do *just that*. Financially enslaving the whole of Germany with their war reparations! As if it was the ordinary Germans that started The Great War. It wasn't just a mistake. It was and, even now, it still remains, clear oppression. *And* a *massive* blunder. Even a *slave* wouldn't take that lying down. Not for long. Hitler's right. It's better to die trying for freedom than to submit to that kind of treatment. The Germans will take the first opportunity to break free. And it will eventually mean that German airships *do* return to bomb London. Only, next time it won't be airships. It will be aircraft. Highly engineered German aircraft."

"Ah well," Monika replied to this nightmarish forecast, "Hitler's popularity is waning now. Let's hope he doesn't win the next German election."

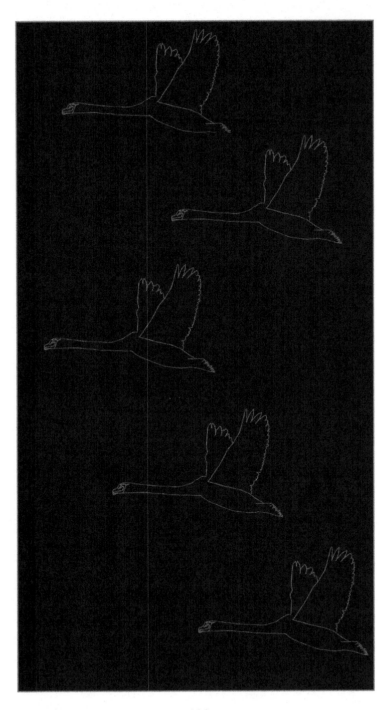

138

"I have repeated my mistake," John said to Monika a few days later. "I allowed my natural goodwill sufficient liberty to attempt a conversation with my family. Seems like a fair thing to try once in a while. Just in case they at last find themselves able to respond. I attempted to tell them about that Tuesday-night political meeting. I mentioned how both the Bolsheviks and the Fascists claim to be struggling towards freedom. But it doesn't always seem to be quite the same freedom. And I asked them, my family, who after all are my very own people, if they had thought about what freedom really is and about what the word really means."

"And what did they say?" Monika asked.

"Absolutely nothing to the point. But Eileen said they had been wondering where I disappear to and asked in a loaded and unpleasant way whether you travel with me when I'm away for two or three nights in a row."

"Oh," Monika responded.

"Of course I said you didn't. And, don't worry, they believed me. Isn't it absurd that we feel uncomfortable about telling the truth even though it is the truth and we know there is nothing to feel uncomfortable about. And even if there were to be anything, even if you did travel with me, it's none of their business anyway. Beyond the matter of whether you were with me or not they were not at all interested in what I was trying to say. It wasn't as if I was trying to convince them of anything. It was just that it seemed an interesting topic to me. Something we might actually *talk* about. But......... it's all just part of their arrogant secrecy. Or pettiness. They want to know everything about me but regard everything about their business as out of bounds to me. And they have no interest in any exchange of ideas, especially of an idealistic kind. None whatsoever. In fact the very mention seems to tire them out. I should have learnt by now not to try to have conversations with them. Do you think it is because Eileen is Jewish?" John asked.

"Absurd ......." Monika echoed distantly. She seemed distracted. "Partly it is because you are young." She reflected for a moment.

"To change the subject," she said in a measured way, "I have the tickets for 'That's a Good Girl' for tomorrow night in London. So bring some overnight things. The trains out of Waterloo are still surprisingly frequent, even after the show."

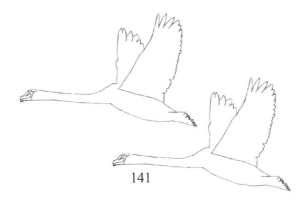

"I think," Eileen said to Eric, "there *must* be a girl somewhere. Why else would John be away from home at night? Although he denied it I had begun to think, like the rest of the village, that he had a liaison with Monika. But it's not Monika. I know because when he was away in Birmingham I bumped into her in Elys. But probably it is *somebody*."

"Oh," Eric replied, "Perhaps you are right. Perhaps there is a girl somewhere. Or maybe he *is* just travelling with the sole purpose of attending meetings and lectures. Either way, I think I shall just let it go. Better to defer to his notions of the privacy of the individual. All things considered. John being no lotus-eater."

Eileen sniffed. "There are meetings and there are meetings," she said.

"Although I still argue with Eileen and my father," John ventured to Monika, "about trivial domestic things, I keep from them the real enormity of thought that grows, day by day, in my mind."

"What enormity?" Monika asked turning away from the washing-up, drying her hands, and leaning against the kitchen wall with her arms clasped behind her back.

"Well," John expanded, "It is the bumptious nature of both Eileen and her son, magnified by the ways of their race, that drive me to seek revenge. I feel that I am a microcosm of the German nation. Like the Germans I have had everything taken from me. My family and my inheritance. Like them my response is to remain active even though dented by defeat. It is this feeling of defeat and dispossession that go, in *any* man, to produce the nothing-to-lose outlook."

"But *there is no comparison*, my boy," Monika said very carefully and soberly. She enclosed him in a close hug. "You have *not* lost everything. You have food to eat and a place to live and one day in the not too distant future you will go away to university. So by most standards you are very fortunate. And then it will be *up to you* to make the most of your life. It must be your policy to do your *very* best at university, and then to use your education to better yourself. You must take absolutely *every bit* of knowledge you can from your teachers and lecturers. In fact your prospects are very good. Actually it would not be unfair to say that in economic terms you are one of the lucky few." She stroked his hair. "You must use your time for positive work, not for revenge. Be creative, not destructive."


"And............" Monika continued, "you see............, you must not make the mistake of assuming disinheritance. You *may* have been disinherited but you have no way of being certain. Making the assumption could actually increase the possibility by making the atmosphere worse at home. That's how these things sometimes work. And.........., no-one on earth can be absolutely certain of inheriting. And.......... even if you were to be disinherited, *you* are not being economically enslaved as the Germans were by the war reparations." Monika drew him to the couch and sat down close beside him. "*You* are a relatively free person," she insisted.

"When I go to political meetings," he said, "and they talk about Jewish financiers and about the world's greatest problem being a de facto semi-secret Jewish state within and above states and spanning national boundaries, then I think of Eileen and her international dealings and that she is Jewish."

"*No*, dearest, *no!*" Monika implored, "you *cannot* go down that road." She looked at John, concern in her eyes.

"We *all* want more money. Whether at an individual or a state level. What matters is how we go about getting it."

"Exactly!" John responded. "You need look no further than Eileen."

"No, no, no, *no*! *sweetheart,*" Monika pleaded, "You do not have to look too hard to see that the English and the French and the Germans, in fact *all* men of *all* nations, are just as avaricious as the Jews have always been accused of being. We are all alike."

John reached out to touch her still damp hand. "You're not Jewish are you, Monika?" he asked.

"No! my love. You know I'm not." She smiled at him.

"Oh well," John sighed. "You are the exact opposite of Eileen. Within your fair mind there is never any *hint* of greed. Exactly the reverse. I think of you as a best friend. My *very* best friend in fact."

"I am glad to be your friend," she said. "I want to be your friend. *For ever*, I want to be your friend. *But*," she asserted, "I think one should never rank friends in terms of best, second best and third best. Rather they are like portraits and still-lifes that come and go from vision and consciousness. A painting may hang upon your wall for many years without being really studied. Friends are like that. And if you really like them they are always with you in one way or another, in the background or sometimes in the foreground, even after they are dead. Just as your mother is always with me. I speak to her every day, you know, even though she has been gone for a while now."

"Come here," John said drawing her into a close embrace.

"Oooh," Monika responded. "That's nice. It's usually me that starts the hugging."

"Yes," he said provocatively. "But this time I noticed your bosom was rising and falling just a little too fast."

"So," he said after a long silence in which the close embrace was not relaxed, "*You* think that I must be at ease with the fact that my father married a Jewess."

"Yes," Monika replied, breaking away to look at him, "most emphatically I do. And you *must*. And...........*peaceably*. Even if things are.........not quite right.......at the moment. Keep in mind that every single person on this planet has faults."

He drew her back in for a brief moment retightening his hug. But then, placing his hands on her shoulders, he held her at arms-length, watching her breathing. "Your bosom is on the move again," he said looking at her intently. "You are so soft and neat and fair. I love you."

"Our lives are difficult enough," Eileen said to Eric, "without still having every single day to put up with all John's nonsense. So? He is spending time away from home and going you know not where? So! *You* take the initiative. *You* fund his exploration! Give him money! Give him the means to put up somewhere safe when he travels. Then you will not have to worry so much about him when he is away. Think of it as money well spent because it will buy us the time and privacy we need to save ourselves. Our own difficulties are great. We do not need them compounded with all this daily turmoil concerning John."

Later that day Eric took his son aside. "Here is money," Eric said. "Use it wisely. I have agreed this with Eileen. We are obviously aware that you are away a lot. We don't know where you go. We know you don't wish to tell us. We do not wish to intrude on your privacy by asking. It will be a monthly allowance. I think it is generous. If you are away from home it could be used to provide accommodation. Of a reasonable standard. We hope you will use it to good educational purpose until the time comes to go to university."

"So, am I now a 'remittance man'?" John studied his father. He took the money. "Compensation?" he asked.

"Well, I don't know," John reflected one evening as, an early autumn chill in the air, he and Monika shared the couch and with their bodily warmth, warmed one-another, "why do we still labour through an age in which dictator and democrat, class and culture are at such odds? Why can't we just be free? Why can't we just live? You tell me, Monika, that I must not fall into any hypnosis such as belonging to a political party or movement. You say sane personal independence is vital. You say no-one should partake of the opium of membership of a cult. So.........how exactly," he asked himself rather than Monika, "and what exactly should any reasonable person think? How should one live? And how behave? Now that we have all reached the present...... And now that we know for certain what The Great War was.............just so much useless wasteful destruction and death."


They were quiet for a while. And then Monika answered. "One might," she said, "no matter how bad or good things are, turn away from politics and look to poetry. The most important thing, my boy, is to hold onto your sanity. You may fail to influence or persuade others. Or you may hold sway. But you are nothing without your sane sovereign mind. In all circumstances, no matter how diverse, from the dire to the fabulous, sanity depends upon keeping alive your faculty of *independent* thought. You must maintain a cordon sanitaire between yourself and that which troubles you. *And* between yourself and that which elates you. Except you may let love in..........and out..... Love," she smiled, "is both sane and insane............. "Because," Monika reverted to her theme, "sanity is itself a necessity for survival. Also it is a companion of happiness. And remember, sometimes it is between the lines of doctrine rather than along the lines, that happiness is found."

"But definitely keep well clear of all cults," Monika continued. "The immense wars that raged in Europe for centuries, usually dynasty against dynasty, or sometimes religion against religion, were little more than cult wars. Started by racketeers, thugs and brigands. For their own profit. I have lost one man in the trenches. I would hate for to see you too caught up in the next episode of all that same *madness*. Do *whatever it takes* to stay out of it. *Far* better that you be your own sovereign self than some politician's pawn. *Conscripted* to carry *his* rifle and shoot at *his* enemy, you know not *why*."

John pondered this. "Better to withdraw into isolation," he mused, "to trek *far* away to some place where it is possible to stand alone. And not be caught up in the mass consciousness of war fever. Or *any* mass consciousness, for that matter...... I have been reading," he said after a pause, "about The Transvaal. A worthy way of life might be led there. Plenty of very cheap land. Masses of space where an individual may be an individual. In The Transvaal the white population is a mixture of British, Dutch and German. They are a people who seem to have learnt a great deal from the disgraceful waste of The Boer Wars. And from the anguish of German East Africa in 1916. *And* from the losses they suffered fighting for the British in France and in German South West Africa. It's astonishing that they fought for Britain at all in The Great War, considering what happened in The Boer Wars. But........ it seems they have learnt their lesson. At last...... So........in the light of their experience they will probably use the power South Africa now has, as a dominion, to remain neutral if the *stupid* Europeans decide to go to war again."

"I don't want you to go so far away," Monika said quickly.

John searched on.

Monika watched and waited. "I often see," she said, "how deep in thought you are. I both want and do not want your independence. I would like to contribute. But...... Somehow....... The best solutions to our vexations are the ones we find ourselves, or invent ourselves. So I try to be available to you, but unintrusive. You must invent *your own* future."

"I know. And......thank you......," John embraced her.

"But secretly," John told himself, "I think I may know the one true way forward. Monika's 'poetry' solution is very attractive. And her belief in existential independence is logical. For the individual it is logical. But *everything* will be lost if the systems that support Western culture and civilisation continue to be swept away. It is too much of an abdication for the individual to neglect *that* responsibility in favour of 'poetry.' The one doctrine that will properly promote western culture in a modern way is self-reliant National Socialism. Of course, this huge hope is something I cannot divulge to Monika. She would be *distraught*. Absolutely beside herself. She is so gentle. And yet, somehow, the name itself rings with logic..... National Socialism...... It is beautiful like wind on long reeds." He thought of a passage he had recently translated from memory, and rather roughly, set down in 'MY TABLES' after visiting a library.

## The Gist of a Paragraph in "Mein Kampf"

### Roughly Translated From Memory a day or two after I visited the library.

'People dare not nowadays recall the high splendour of our past achievements, so magnificent then was our culture. For, in our time, by sharp contrast, the result of the wrongful capitulation of our erstwhile princes, all that is left us is our misery.'

"And yet......." he continued to soliloquise, "I am just *not* ready to commit. I definitely must study this thing closely. Am I looking at chaos? Or am I looking at perfect order? God! Someone pass me my opera glasses. Out of self-respect I need to know more. For me it's either going to be National Socialism or its going to be migration to somewhere like South Africa. Those are the choices before me.

Perhaps," his thoughts drifted........., "my hesitation comes from Monika. From what she thinks. She says it is quite usual for a woman to teach the man of her choice how she would be loved........ And she teaches me........And we hesitate........And are not lovers. But we love one another. We *could* be lovers. She influences me a great deal. Oh *God*, I crave the tonic of belonging. Just the internal happiness of belonging. To someone, or something. *Why is it so obscure?"*

Out loud, he said to Monika, "I want somehow to use the allowance my father gives me to search beyond all the immediate and terrific events of our times for some higher way to live. Somewhere in history, literature, philosophy, mathematics even, possibly music, there will be some idea or remedy that might be brought to bear. So far I have found only false trails, unpalatable truths. Any hatred I feel is too shallow to fit in with some of the current fierce ideologies............. I imagine I will know the solution when I see it."

"Good," she said, "Good. Keep going. Tell me more."

"I am trying to convert academic thought into practicality," he revealed hesitantly. "I want not just to read books, but also to be able to read faces and bodies, to be able to see into and through them. Into souls. I want to be able to know people for what they *are*." He paused. "If I have found anything it is that, sacred or profane, the lives people actually lead are very different from the lives the world sees. Or is allowed to see. People are secretive. As often as not one man's freedom leads to another man's imprisonment."

"Yes," Monika agreed. "And we are hemmed in by the time-dimension. We are granted only 'threescore years and ten' in which to search. In which to see the good and the bad. Time itself is both a freedom and a boundary. In our one little lifetime we must not squander time or freedom. We must use every minute...... So....... Assemble as much knowledge as you can, my boy. And when you are not engaged in loving, at least be engaged in living well."

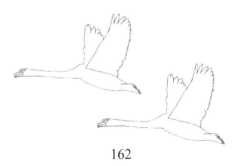

It was a Sunday evening. The time for going away to university loomed. The cups and plates were clean and dry and put away. As was their habit they were sitting close together, sharing their warmth. They looked through the French windows, admiring the tidiness of their garden. In that year of genteel labouring they had sewn the seed and nursed the seedling, trained creeper and branch, seen off snail and insect, brought blossom and fruit. Now they rested, sharing once more, for many minutes, a peaceable silence. The autumn pruning had begun. Winter was not that far off. The university would tear them apart. They considered the possibilities of their togetherness just as they considered the borders of their flower-beds. It was unspoken. All was still. Surely the threat was not real! Fate would *not* be so unkind as to part them! Surely? Something must be *done*. Something that would preserve the well-being they had made. Some act was needed. A confirmation. John turned slightly. It was time. He placed a masculine hand on a lacy shoulder. Monika's breathing quickened. She sat quite still. Time halted. One by one, steadily, her buttons were undone. She looked into his face. He crossed several Rubicons until his palm reached warm skin.

"John," Monika's voice was kind, "you can if you wish. I give you permission. You may do anything to me. Anything at all. I will do anything you ask. But I have to tell you. If we become lovers we shall not continue friends in the same way. Our love will be intense. But it will not last. And neither will our friendship. Because love of this kind changes everything. Especially when there is an age difference such as there is between thee and me. So....... if you decide to withdraw your hand now, it will mean that we shall always be friends. And....... instead of precious friendship being soon lost, we shall keep a precious certainty." She paused. "But truly, it is completely your choice. If you think the moment has come and the prize is worth it, and that instead of everlasting friendship you would like always to have in your memory a complete knowledge of me, then I am your most, most willing accomplice. But it is fully your choice. You must be the *man*. You decide. This is the very moment at which you choose what, in future, we will be to one another. Which kind of forever it will be."

John froze. With a farewell caress he withdrew his hand. Uncertain what to do he clumsily rebuttoned her blouse, straightened her clothing. Fearful of misinterpretation he kept close. "I choose perpetual friendship," he said heavily. Adjusting slightly, they embraced. And there they remained watching the autumn dusk turn dark. In the night they stirred to attend to nature, quickly returning to the warmth of their closeness. "God," John murmured in comic half-sleep, "you tip-toe *so* loudly." By way of reply Monika snuggled into him more nearly. "And you," she said, "should aim straight." In the morning, still dressed, they were at peace. They made breakfast.

"Just as well," Monika smiled at him when he left. "I am just *so* much older than you. I believe there is more to you, my boy, than any single person on this earth will ever know."

"When we speak of last night, what happened........or didn't happen, let's call it 'our closeness'," John suggested. "It will be our secret code........ for many possibilities. All of which, I think, *remain*."

Still John searched. "Some artists and scientists," he said to Monika, "are driven mad by their work. But some have the sense to just plod on."

"The ones I admire," Monika responded, "are those who turn the tables on awfulness, those who manage not only to confront awfulness, but actually to harness the energy of their own desperation and use the harnessed energy to carve out success."

"I have been carrying this around for a while now," he said handing her a piece of paper on which he had copied out 'Nuances and Subtleties,' his poem to her. "Until now I haven't plucked up courage to give it to you. But, 'come what come may,' and with trepidation, here it is."

A few weeks after their 'closeness', John made an entry in his "TABLES" about a girl. Sitting at Monika's desk, he turned to the next blank page and in keeping with his format, wrote a title and set to work.

## "A GIRL IN A GOLD AND ORANGE ROOM."

"A vision of wit closed in,
    her whiteness bringing
the velvet glimpse
    and slender longing.

But a startled hinterland
    of care declined
her gold and scarlet
    world outlined. "

After much rethinking and much use of the eraser he was semi-satisfied. He re-read his words many times thinking they might, some day, come in useful.

After a while he closed the book and put it back in its drawer. And then he sat back and thought.

"So," he thought, "this is how women are. Whenever there is an encounter, the woman holds the man in her aura, and there he is held strongly or less strongly, until the next woman succeeds. The next woman is a new realm and she changes the aura to her own. This is a war between women. Men are mere poetic conscripts. Women encourage the world to think them powerless, but there are spheres in which women hold the cards. Or most of them. Especially at the outset."

John told Monika about the girl he had met in a library. "I want to tell you about a girl in an orange room," he said.

Monika listened intently, her forehead creased. "I am glad you took my advice," she said, and hugged him tightly for a long time. "And I am glad that my writ ran during your debut. It kept you safe. And it seems to me as I look at you now that my writ still runs. Come," she said, when she unclasped him, "lets go up to London for lunch and to the pictures. There's a Charlie Chaplin film called 'The Circus' on at the picture houses. I met Mrs Leech in the village yesterday and she said it is very good. And I have found a very nice place we can go on to for a special dinner afterwards. It's quite posh and has only recently opened."

## AUTHORS' NOTE

Of the eighty-three chapters planned for 'A Sound of Swans Flying' the following two are now available in electronic and paper versions.

CHAPTER 1      'Vygie'

CHAPTER 2      'Monika'

# REQUEST

Dear Reader,

If you have found anything of interest in this chapter, please leave a review on Amazon. Your thoughts will be studied by Lucille and myself. This is the second of the 83 chapters we plan. My chapters will be those set predominantly in England. Lucille is writing the South African chapters. But there will be overlap...... We *more or less* agree on where we are headed!

Thank you.
James H.

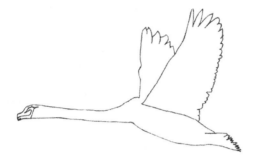

Printed in Great Britain
by Amazon

78960038R00103